A Note to Parents

Eyewitness Readers is a compelling new program for beginning readers, designed in conjunction with leading literacy experts, including Dr. Linda Gambrell, President of the National Reading Conference and past board member of the International Reading Association.

Eyewitness has become the most trusted name in illustrated books, and this new series combines the highly visual *Eyewitness* approach with engaging, easy-to-read stories. Each *Eyewitness Reader* is guaranteed to capture a child's interest while developing his or her reading skills, general knowledge, and love of reading.

The four levels of *Eyewitness Readers* are aimed at different reading abilities, enabling you to choose the books that are exactly right for your children:

Level 1, for **Preschool to Grade 1**
Level 2, for **Grades 1 to 3**
Level 3, for **Grades 2 and 3**
Level 4, for **Grades 2 to 4**

The "normal" age at which a child begins to read can be anywhere from three to eight years old, so these levels are intended only as a general guideline.

No matter which level you select, you can be sure that you are helping your child learn to read, then read to learn!

A DK PUBLISHING BOOK
www.dk.com

Senior Editor Linda Esposito
Senior Art Editor Andrew Burgess
Managing Art Editor Peter Bailey
US Editor Regina Kahney
Production Josie Alabaster
Photography John Daniels
Reading Consultant
Linda B. Gambrell, Ph.D.

First American Edition, 1999
2 4 6 8 10 9 7 5 3 1
Published in the United States by
DK Publishing, Inc.
95 Madison Avenue, New York, New York 10016

Published in Great Britain by Dorling Kindersley Limited.

Library of Congress Cataloging-in-Publication Data
Wallace, Karen
      Duckling Days / written by Karen Wallace.
      p.   cm. -- (Eyewitness readers. Level 1)
      Summary: A mother duck builds her nest, lays her eggs, hatches
six ducklings, and teaches them about life on their own.
ISBN 0-7894-3994-8 (pb) -- ISBN 0-7894-3995-6 (hc)
      1. Ducks--Infancy--Juvenile literature. [1. Ducks.
2. Animals--Infancy.] I. Title. II. Series.
      QL696.A52W33   1999   JE
      598.4'1139--dc21
                                                                98-41846
                                                                       CIP
                    WAL   AC
                     c.1
      Color reproduction by Colourscan, Singapore
            Printed and bound in Belgium by Proost

The publisher would like to thank the following for
their kind permission to reproduce their photographs:
a=above; c=center; b=below/bottom; l=left;
r=right; t=top

Barrie Watts:
5cr, 6b, 7tr, 26cl (below), 26cl, 27c (below),
27r, 28cl (above)

$12.95

EYEWITNESS ◉ READERS

Level
1
PRESCHOOL-GRADE 1

Duckling Days

Written by Karen Wallace

DK PUBLISHING, INC.
www.dk.com

In the grass
beside the river
a mother duck
builds her nest.

She gathers grass and makes a hollow.

She lines her nest with downy feathers.

nest

In a nest
beside the river
a mother duck
lays six white eggs.

egg

She keeps them warm
beneath her body.
Inside each egg
a duckling grows.

A duckling hatches
from his egg.

shell

He cracks the shell.

He makes a hole
with his tiny beak.

He taps and pushes.

He breaks out of the shell
and squeezes out.

Other ducklings
hatch beside him.
At first their legs
are weak and wobbly.

Their downy feathers
are wet and sticky.
They dry out quickly
near their mother.

Mother duck has
six fluffy ducklings.
She leads them down
toward the river.

One little duckling
is left behind.

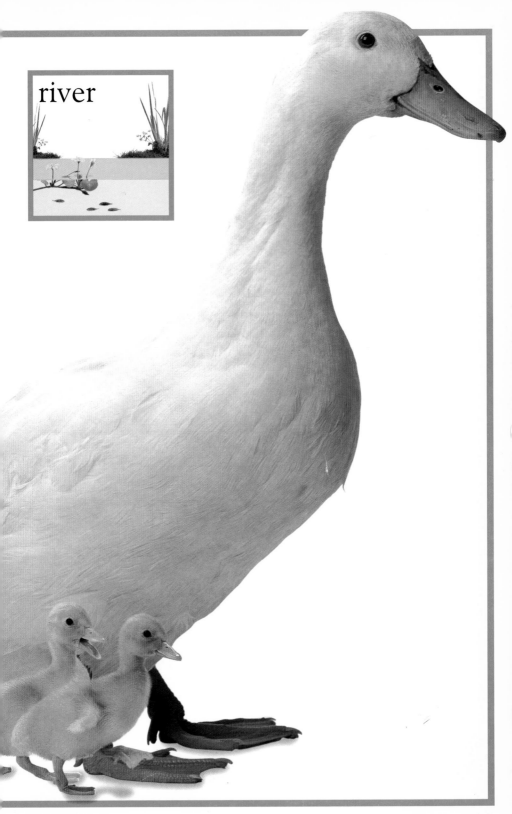

river

13

cheep
cheep

One little duckling
cheeps and twitters.
Where is his mother?

Where can
she be?

The little duckling
runs to find her.

cheep

He's afraid to be
on his own.

Five ducklings jump
into the water.
They push and paddle
with webbed feet.

webbed
feet

cheep

The little duckling
finds his family.

Mother duck checks
her ducklings.

Six fluffy babies
swim beside her.

In the river
the water is deep.
Mother duck dives
and leaves her ducklings.

She nibbles plants.
She chases beetles.

19

Six little ducklings
look around them.

Where is mother duck?
Where can she be?

cheep

cheep

cheep

Cheep! Cheep!
The ducklings call for mother.

cheep

cheep

cheep

A bee buzzes in the air.

bzzzzzzzzzzzzzzzZZZZ ZZZZZZZ ZZZZ ZZZZZ ZZZZ

A frog croaks from a lily pad.

croak

Two birds sing on a branch.

tweet tweet

But mother duck
does not answer.
Where has she gone?
Where can she be?

Quack! Quack!
She pops up in the water!

quack

quack

cheep

cheep

cheep

Cheep! Cheep!
Her ducklings huddle around her.

Next time
they will be braver.

cheep

cheep

cheep

The growing ducklings
snap at tadpoles.
They pull at pondweed
with their yellow bills.

bill

They like to dabble
in the water.

They watch their mother.
They do what she does.

The ducklings' down
grows into feathers.

feathers

They watch
their mother clean
her feathers.

She flaps and fluffs.

She plucks
and preens.

She strokes
and smooths.

Mother duck
is combed
and clean!

29

Five young ducks waddle
from the river.

They shake the water
from their backs.
They flap their wings
just like their mother.
They clean their feathers
with their beaks.

wing

One young duck
dabbles in the water.
He's happy being
on his own.

Picture Word List

nest

page 5

webbed feet
page 16

egg

page 6

bill

page 26

shell
page 8

feathers
page 28

river

page 13

wing
page 30

EYEWITNESS ◉ READERS

Level 1 *Beginning to Read*

A Day at Greenhill Farm
Truck Trouble
Tale of a Tadpole
Surprise Puppy!
Duckling Days
A Day at Seagull Beach

Level 2 *Beginning to Read Alone*

Dinosaur Dinners
Fire Fighter!
Bugs! Bugs! Bugs!
Slinky, Scaly Snakes!
Animal Hospital
The Little Ballerina

Level 3 *Reading Alone*

Spacebusters
Beastly Tales
Shark Attack!
Titanic
Invaders from Outer Space
Movie Magic

Level 4 *Proficient Readers*

Days of the Knights
Volcanoes
Secrets of the Mummies
Pirates!
Horse Heroes
The Wooden Horse

AAV - 8812